D1385465

For David and Amelia
M.W.

For Charlie
B.F.

First published 1991 by
Walker Books Ltd
87 Vauxhall Walk
London SE11 5HJ

This edition published 2001

2 4 6 8 10 9 7 5 3

Text © 1991 Martin Waddell
Illustrations © 1991 Barbara Firth

Printed in Singapore

British Library Cataloguing in Publication Data:
a catalogue record for this book
is available from the British Library

ISBN 0-7445-8172-9

LET'S GO HOME, LITTLE BEAR

Written by
Martin Waddell

Illustrated by
Barbara Firth

WALKER BOOKS
AND SUBSIDIARIES
LONDON • BOSTON • SYDNEY

Once there were two bears.
Big Bear and Little Bear.
Big Bear is the big bear
and Little Bear is the little bear.
They went for a walk in the woods.

They walked and they walked and
they walked until Big Bear said,
"Let's go home, Little Bear."
So they started back home on the
path through the woods.

P L O D   P L O D   P L O D
went Big Bear, plodding along.
Little Bear ran on in front,
jumping and sliding
and having great fun.

And then…
Little Bear stopped
and he listened
and then he turned round
and he looked.

"Come on, Little Bear," said Big Bear,
 but Little Bear didn't stir.
"I thought I heard something!" Little Bear said.
"What did you hear?" said Big Bear.
"Plod, plod, plod," said Little Bear.
"I think it's a Plodder!"
 Big Bear turned round and
 he listened and looked.
 No Plodder was there.
"Let's go home, Little Bear," said Big Bear.
"The plod was my feet in the snow."

They set off again on the path
through the woods.
P L O D   P L O D   P L O D
went Big Bear with Little Bear
walking beside him,
just glancing a bit, now and again.

And then…
Little Bear stopped
and he listened
and then he turned round
and he looked.

"Come on, Little Bear," said Big Bear,
  but Little Bear didn't stir.
"I thought I heard something!"
  Little Bear said.
"What did you hear?" said Big Bear.
"Drip, drip, drip," said Little Bear.
"I think it's a Dripper!"

Big Bear turned round, and
he listened and looked.
No Dripper was there.
"Let's go home, Little Bear,"
said Big Bear.
"That was the ice as it
dripped in the stream."

They set off again on the
path through the woods.
P L O D   P L O D   P L O D
went Big Bear with Little Bear
closer beside him.

And then...
Little Bear stopped
and he listened
and then he turned round
and he looked.

"Come on, Little Bear," said Big Bear,
 but Little Bear didn't stir.
"I know I heard something this time!"
 Little Bear said.
"What did you hear?" said Big Bear.
"Plop, plop, plop," said Little Bear.
"I think it's a Plopper."

Big Bear turned round,
and he listened and looked.
No Plopper was there.
"Let's go home, Little Bear,"
said Big Bear.
"That was the snow plopping
down from a branch."

PLOD PLOD PLOD
went Big Bear along the path
through the woods.
But Little Bear walked
slower and slower
and at last he sat
down in the snow.

"Come on, Little Bear," said Big Bear.
"It is time we were both back home."
But Little Bear sat and said nothing.
"Come on and be carried,"
said Big Bear.

Big Bear put Little Bear
high up on his back,
and set off down the path
through the woods.

WOO WOO WOO
"It is only the wind, Little Bear,"
said Big Bear and he walked
on down the path.

CREAK CREAK CREAK
"It is only the trees, Little Bear,"
said Big Bear and he walked
on down the path.

PLOD   PLOD   PLOD
"It is only the sound of my feet
again," said Big Bear,
and he plodded on and on
and on until they came
back home to their cave.

Big Bear and Little Bear
went down into the dark,
the dark of their own
Bear Cave.

"Just stay there, Little Bear,"
said Big Bear, putting Little Bear
in the Bear Chair with a blanket
to keep him warm.
Big Bear stirred up the fire
from the embers
and lighted the lamps
and made the Bear Cave
all cosy again.
"Now tell me a story,"
Little Bear said.

And Big Bear sat down in the Bear Chair
with Little Bear curled on his lap.
And he told a story of Plodders
and Drippers and Ploppers
and the sounds of the snow
in the woods,
and this Little Bear
and this Big Bear
plodding all the way…

HOME